# Richard Scarry's
# BUSIEST
# FIRE FIGHTERS
# EVER!

## A GOLDEN BOOK • NEW YORK

Western Publishing Company, Inc., Racine, Wisconsin 53404

Sparky, Smokey, Snozzle, and Squirty are
fire fighters at the Busytown Fire Station.

They are always ready to
help the people of Busytown.

The fire fighters do not just put out fires. They help solve all kinds of problems.

When Hilda loses her house keys down the drain in the street, Smokey pulls them out with a magnet.

When Pig Won't climbs a tree and goes too high, Sparky, Snozzle, and Squirty bring him back down again.

The fire fighters remove branches
that fall on Mr. Frumble's car.

They also remove earth that falls
on Mr. Frumble's car.

Oops!

Finally they remove Mr. Frumble's car.

If the fire alarm rings, the fire fighters are always ready to go. The fire engine is always clean. The hoses and tools are always in order.

Mr. Frumble sees smoke rising in the garden next door.

He runs to the fire alarm
box and pulls the handle.
The alarm bell rings
at the fire station.

In an instant Smokey, Sparky, Snozzle, and
Squirty slide down the pole to their fire engine.
They speed off through the streets of Busytown.

The bell clangs.
The siren blares.

Look out, everyone!

There's Mr. Frumble!
There's the smoke!

Smokey hooks up the fire engine to the fire hydrant.

Sparky and Squirty unravel the hose.
Snozzle runs ahead with the nozzle.

SSSWWWIIISSSHHH!
SSCCHHWWAASSHH!!
SWOOOSH!!!

The Greenbug family was having
a barbecue. Out goes the fire.
Oh, dear.

The fire fighters take the Greenbug family and Mr. Frumble back to the firehouse for a fire fighter barbecue.

Fire fighters know how
to make good fires as well
as how to put out bad fires!